ALL THE WAYS TO BE SMART

Davina Bell & Allison Colpoys

SCRIBBLE

To dearest Belle,
the inspiration for this book,
thank you.
Love, Aunty Al

To dear Harry and Oscar, Sammy, Noah and Christopher,
Scarlett, Rapha and Lucy, Rose, Magnolia and Voss, Georgie, James
and Ben, Sophie, Thomas and William, Max, Genevieve and Charlotte,
Indi and Camille, Hugo and Angus, Fergus, Clover and Charlotte.
You are all so smart!
Love, Aunty Beans

And to dear Esther,
we can't wait to see
all the ways you are smart.
Love, Al & Davina

The author and illustrator would like to say a heartfelt thank you to
Jeremy Wortsman and Lorelei Vashti for having us to stay at Jacky Winter Gardens,
where many ideas for this book were dreamed up.

The illustrations in this book were made
with ink, charcoal and pencil and digitally assembled

Typeset in Gill Sans

Published by Scribble, an imprint of Scribe Publications
2018 (Australia) and 2019 (UK and US)
Reprinted 2018 (twice), 2019 (four times), 2020 (four times), 2021 (twice)

18–20 Edward Street, Brunswick, Victoria 3056, Australia
2 John Street, Clerkenwell, London, WC1N 2ES, United Kingdom
3754 Pleasant Ave, Suite 100, Minneapolis, Minnesota 55409 USA

Text © Davina Bell, 2018
Illustrations © Allison Colpoys, 2018

This book is printed with vegetable-soy based inks, on FSC certified
paper from responsibly managed forests, ensuring that the supply chain
from forest to end-user is chain of custody certified

Printed and bound in Poland by Ozgraf

MIX
Paper from
responsible sources
FSC
www.fsc.org   FSC® C163799

978 1 925713 43 5 (Australian hardback)
978 1911617 55 6 (UK hardback)
978 1911617 87 7 (UK paperback)
978 1947534 96 4 (North American hardback)

Catalogue records for this title are available from the
National Library of Australia and the British Library

scribblekidsbooks.com

I can't wait to share with you
how smart you are the whole day through.

Smart at drawing witches' hats,
smart at gluing wings on bats.

Smart at rhyme and telling time,
and building cubbies, making slime.

Smart is not just ticks and crosses,
smart is building boats from boxes.

Painting patterns, wheeling wagons,
being mermaids, riding dragons.

Smart at drawing things with claws,
facts about the dinosaurs.
Folding aeroplanes for flying…

Smart is kindness when there's crying.

Growing, throwing, bubble blowing.

Smart is knowing where you're going.

Finding treasures, flower picking…

Ukulele!

Finger clicking!

Smart at sharing, caring, scaring,
smart at picking what you're wearing.

Smart at saying hi and bye

to people when they feel all shy.

Smart is reading,
writing, spelling,
but it's also
storytelling.

Finding things on all the pages…

sitting still and quiet for ages.

Smart is not
just being best
at spelling bees,
a tricky test.

Or knowing all
the answers ever…

Other things
are just as clever.

Every hour of every day,
we're smart in our
own special way.

And nobody
will ever do…

the very same smart things as you.